The Werewolf

Meets His Match

Paranormal Wolf Shifter Romance

Abby Raine

ISBN: 1508829942
ISBN-13: 978-1508829942

DEDICATION

To all the lovers out there that think and know there is something more...

CONTENTS

CHAPTER 1

Eliza Stark had always been afraid of the dark. She knew there was no rational reason for fearing darkness—she knew it because people kept telling her. "Stop shaking like a little girl," an ex-lover had said once, as they'd gone through the ghost train in an amusement park. "There's nothing here that can really hurt you. It's just dark. What are you... a baby?" It was not hard to work out why he was an ex-lover.

She had always jumped at shadows, and had been terrified to be left in a dark room alone. She knew this was quite a common fear, and so derived no sense of uniqueness from it. But even so it defined her. Her fear of darkness was like a blanket with which she wrapped herself and made up her character: she was, at heart, a dark-fearer.

Once, when she was walking home alone at night – something she hated to do, but something that was sometimes necessary – all the streetlamps had gone off. Later, she had learnt that a blackout had affected the whole street and some of the adjoining neighborhoods. But at the time she had been oblivious of this fact, and she had wept. For a twenty-seven-year-old woman, weeping because it was dark was embarrassing. Immediately, the thoughts started: What is wrong with you, are you a baby, you need to get yourself together, you're a grown woman... And on and on and on.

She was sure that was why she latched onto him; he was the only safe presence in that dark place.
******

She worked for an insurance company and was working through a back-log of complaints one night when she realized that time had sped away from her: it was receding into Tomorrow Land, already. She looked outside and saw the moon shining its inadequate rays upon the suddenly terrifying street below. She looked around her office and realized that everybody else had left, most likely hours ago. She had been in a pin-point focus-mode where everything in her peripheries had paled to nonexistence and all she knew were those lines and lines of complaints. Now her concentration had been broken and she was alone.

Like any twenty-first-century person who works in an office, Eliza didn't know all of her co-workers. There were the ones who worked on her floor, with whom she was acquainted, and there were the occasional ones she remembered, like the mail-boy who was always polite to her, but beyond that her eight-story office might as well have been comprised of one room alone. Now, in this darkness, she saw a man she had never seen before.
He was tall with blonde, short hair with the sides shaved. With that haircut – and, as he got closer, with his blue-grey eyes – he looked like a Viking.

The hair on top was tied in a knot with something that looked like twine— that looked primitive and out-of-place.
He was walking through the office when Eliza did something that was so out of character afterwards she would not be able to justify it.
She called across the office: "Hello."
The man stopped, and his head snapped to her. It snapped so violently that for moment she thought he was going to scream at her, or else attack her— all illogical things to think, but darkness was here now (unless you counted that pathetic electric lights that tried, unsuccessfully, to replace daylight).

The man looked expectantly at Eliza. Eliza hadn't planned this far – she hadn't planned at all – and so was now at a loss for what to say.
She repeated, stupidly: "Hello."
The man tilted his head at her, like a predator examining its prey, and then replied: "Hello."
He walked across the office to where she sat and looked down at her. "Do I know you?"

"No," she said, and her cheeks reddened. "I don't know why I said "hello" now." She let out an embarrassed giggle. "It's weird, isn't it? Because we don't know each other? I'm just... I don't like... No one is here. I just thought because—you're here, and I'm here." He was looking at her intently now. He had faint blonde stubble on his face and his eyes were penetrative: Eliza had the feeling of being looked at, through, and into all at once. "I just thought—" She trailed off again. She finished weakly: "Manners, you know."

The man smiled, which set Eliza at ease somewhat. His teeth were white and well-cared-for. Eliza had a pointless image of him in a Viking rowing boat, moving the oar through the water with his powerful arms. And they were powerful. She could see that now he was closer. He wore a shirt with the sleeves rolled up. His forearms bulged and his shirt was tight around the biceps. But what she liked most was he didn't seem to know he was attractive or muscular. He wasn't one of those look-at-me-I-go-to-the-gym-aren't-I-sexy men.

"Manners, yes," the man said. His accent was Irish. His voice was deep. "My name is Gregory Fitzgerald. It's nice to meet you."
He held out his hand. They shook, and Eliza told him her name. His hand was bigger than hers, and seemed to envelop it; and it was warm; and beneath it Eliza could sense, more than feel, the strength, the dormant strength. She knew this was a hand that could exert dangerous force if it wanted.

"I'm just here doing some boring office-work shit," Gregory said. "What about you?"
"Same," Eliza said.
"It's fun, isn't it? Staying here until—" He looked at his watch. "Until ten p.m. to get some work done you aren't even interested in?"
"You don't like your job?"
He looked around at the walls and the desks and the pillars that held up the close ceiling above, and his eyebrows furrowed. "It's too far from nature," he said.

Eliza didn't know how to respond to that. She didn't know if it was a joke or just a general observation. She made to laugh, and then thought better of it and smiled instead—smiled in a way she hoped said, "I know exactly what you mean."
"I'm nearly done, anyway," Gregory said.

"Me, too," Eliza said.

She knew it was foolish to feel safe just because this man was here. The mere fact that this man happened to be employed by the same company as her did not instantly instill within him a sense of decency and honor. He could've easily been an axe-murderer or rapist. He could easily be one of those men you read about in the newspapers. And just because he was handsome — and he was handsome — he was not exempt from these possibilities. But even so Eliza felt her fears departing.

Gregory sat on the desk chair opposite her and looked out of the window, at the moon. It was an almost-full moon.

"Full moon in two days," Gregory said. He made an odd face. Eliza couldn't decipher it. It was somewhere between excitement and sadness; and Eliza would've denied that such a face could've existed had it not just been made before her.

"Is it?" Eliza said, lightly.

"Yes," Gregory said. "Yes, it is."

There was a pause then, and a semi-silence — it had started to rain, and the light pat-pat-pat against the glass was the only noise — and then Gregory looked her straight in the eyes. Eliza wasn't the most attractive girl. She was short with blonde hair, which men seemed to like. But her breasts weren't huge and she wasn't fond of too much makeup. She had a tattoo of an angel on her upper-chest, just above her breasts, which she now regretted. But when Gregory looked at her, she felt attractive. She searched for a word to describe what she saw in him. She didn't have to search very hard: hunger.

"I need to go," Eliza said.

"Me, too," Gregory said.

There was another pause.

Then Gregory said: "Can I walk you home?"

Any thinking person in this situation would say no. That was what Eliza had been taught since she was a girl. Stranger equals bad. But now she found herself considering the request. And as she considered it, it seemed like the safest option. In the dark, anything could happen to her. With Gregory, she would be safe. He wouldn't do anything.

We all lie to ourselves to justify our choices, Eliza thought, in an attempt to justify the choice she was about to make. And this is my lie: fate has brought Gregory to me, on this night. If Gregory wasn't here I would stabbed in an alleyway tonight. But because he is here I will be safe and everything will be okay.

"Okay," Eliza said, not giving herself any more time to think.

THE WEREWOLF MEETS HIS MATCH

CHAPTER 2

They walked through the night. They didn't stand close to each other at first. There seemed to be an unspoken agreement that Gregory would not crowd her so she did not misinterpret his actions. He seemed acutely aware of her fears, as though he could smell them, like some new-age people believed. When she moved closer to him, as they walked through an underpass, he accepted this and moved closer to her. But he didn't touch her, and for that she was grateful.

She knew that here, in this underpass – with the graffiti-covered walls and the dripping rain that pooled at the sides – Gregory could jump on her. She knew that this was the place where any aspiring rapist would make his move. It was the perfect location; and he could even drag her away after he had clubbed and bashed her. She knew – on some level of her mind, anyway – that these were morbid thoughts. But this was who Eliza was at night. In the day she laughed and she joked and she was perfectly normal; when night came she was a paranoid delusion-monger.

So when they passed through the underpass and came out on the other side, greeted by the rain and the streetlamps, she breathed a sigh of relief. They had said little to each other. As they came out in the open and Eliza knew that he was no longer a threat, she said: "So, what do you do in the company, Gregory?"

"Nothing exciting," he said. "Do you really want to talk about work?"

In fact, she did not want to talk about work, but that was the accepted social norm, wasn't it? Eliza had never been the most socially adept person. Maybe this is why I'm afraid of the dark, she thought, not for the first time. I am scared of the dark because it is unknown, but the darkness that comes at night is a bright summer's day compared to the darkness behind people's public faces—behind the masks they wear most of the time. She knew that these thoughts sounded weird, but even so there was some truth in them. She found it hard to pierce people's exteriors; and the night's darkness only reminded her of that. Or maybe that was all nonsense, and it was only fear of ghouls that made her shiver.

"What do you want to talk about?" she said.

Gregory crossed to the other side of her as they came upon the sidewalk, so he was walking beside the road. Eliza liked this. There was something beautifully old-fashioned about it. "Anything," Gregory said. "Tell me about yourself."

Eliza never knew how to respond to this question. Did she tell him what she ate for breakfast this morning, or what her deepest, darkest urges were? "You'll have to be more specific," she said.

"Tell me a story from your childhood."

"That's a strange request."

"People say they talk to get to know each other, but most of us only learn surface details that are of no importance. 'What's your favorite color?' Blah-blah-blah. But color preference isn't what a person is made of. Neither is favorite food."

"So what is a person made of?"

"Memories. Now, tell me a story."

"Why do you want to get to know me?"

"Tell me a story," Gregory repeated, and now there was a firmness in his voice Eliza found hard to ignore. It was as though she had been pressed against the wall. But she was still walking, one heeled shoe moving and another heeled shoe following through the rainy, cloudy night.

"From my childhood?"

"Yes."

"Okay," Eliza said. She took a deep breath, and searched her mind for an appropriate memory. Then she realized that there was no appropriate memory, for this was not a normal conversation. Gregory had already set the conversation apart from others by declaring other people surface, which Eliza found mildly offensive. Was she, then, surface? She didn't think on this too long—

Gregory was staring at her as they walked, his mouth set in a firm line, his eyes narrowed intently. She felt more than a bit threatened, but did not tell him so. Whether this was because she really liked being looked at like that or she was too scared, she wasn't sure. He was too proud to say I'm waiting, Eliza thought, but it was clear in the way he looked at her.

Eliza cleared her throat and told him the first story she could remember.
******

She had been seven when she'd seen the Dark Man. The Dark Man had come into her house and messed with the things in the kitchen. Her parents had gone down to investigate, and had returned to her bedroom and said there was nothing down there. But Eliza knew they were lying, or at least half-lying. Because there had been something down there.

Before the pots and pans had been disturbed – clattering and clunking, waking everybody in the house – Eliza had been looking out her window, at the stars. As a girl, she had often done this. There were no philosophical musings at that age, but there was a faint impression of something larger than herself, and far from scaring her, this comforted her.

Then a flicker at the bottom of her vision made her look down, and she saw the Dark Man walking through the night, towards her house. She knew she should've said something to her parents, but she was too scared. So she hid under her covers until the clanking started and her parents went down to investigate.

After, her mother sat on the side of her bed and rubbed her hair until she felt asleep, murmuring about how she had just had a bad dream and there had been no Dark Man. But Eliza knew, she always knew, and from that day the dark had always terrified her.

*****

"I know now that it was most likely a burglar," Eliza said. "But if anything that's scarier. It's not hard to work out what happened. My parents must've left the door open – probably by accident – and he had come in and tried to steal something. But he had clattered the pots, and so he ran. I bet my parents found the door open. I asked my mother once, when I was older, and she wouldn't answer. This is how I know something happened that night."

"And you've been afraid of the dark ever since?" Gregory said.

"Yes," Eliza answered, realizing that she was giving much of herself away to this stranger.

She was glad when she rounded the corner and saw her apartment building. She was sad, too, though that was an emotion that lay underneath her gladness. She wanted to get away from this mysterious man because he seemed to have an ability to probe deep inside of her and extract things she never would've normally shared in a situation like this; and she wanted to stay with him for the same reason. She never got to share herself like this. Her mind was a civil war in that moment.

But, as always, she chose the safer option.

"This is my building," she said. "Thank you for walking me home."

They stood facing each other for a few moments, and then, so abruptly Eliza didn't know what was happening until it was happening, Gregory lurched forward and grabbed the back of her head. He pressed his lips against hers, and to her surprise she found herself responding to him. She breathed deeply as they kissed, and his hands moved through her hair and his hard body pressed against hers.

When he let her go, she was panting.

"No problem," Gregory said, and turned away. "I hope to see you again."

"Yes," Eliza breathed. "Yes, me, too."

Then he was gone, into the night, and Eliza was left on her own. When she was back in her apartment, she found it difficult to believe that what had happened was real; surely she had dreamt it. She wasn't the sort of girl who kissed strangers in the night. And, normally, if a stranger had jumped her – and that was what he'd done, wasn't it? – she wouldn't have responded with lust. But she couldn't deny the heat between her legs, the hungry heat, the wanting heat, the heat that told her if this man were to walk into her apartment right now, she would be unsure of her actions.

She tried to resist the urge for a long time. Somehow, it felt wrong. But then she couldn't resist anymore. She took off her tights and her skirt and lay on her bed with her vibrator. She put it inside of herself and imagined the kiss—relived the kiss. She felt his hands in her hair and the warmth and the hardness of his body, and her body writhed and she came, hard.

When she was done she lay on her side and closed her eyes. Gregory filled her vision, and she wanted to know more about him, and to spend more time with him. She hoped he'd meant it when he said he wanted to see her again.

She was too relaxed and tired to be afraid. For once, her sleep was deep and undisturbed.

CHAPTER 3

It had been a Wednesday when Gregory had walked her home. Now it was the Thursday, and Eliza thought that all day she wouldn't see him. She looked for him in the office, looking up every time she heard someone walk across the office floor. It wasn't him. It was just other men and women who worked there, and sometimes they caught her eye. Some of them scowled – mostly women – and some of them smiled – mostly men – but she swiftly looked back down at her desk at every one of them. They weren't who she was interested in.

She worked through the whole day like this. Thankfully, she had caught up with her work the night before, and didn't have to stay late again. This was a good thing, because she hated the dark, hated the Dark Man, and feared one day he would return. But it was also a bad thing, because her meeting with Gregory had taken place in the dark: maybe history would repeat itself. But she wasn't going to stay behind solely to wait for a man who she didn't know, and who may or may not show up. So when the hands on the clock ticked closer and closer to 5.p.m., Eliza got more nervous with each tick, that seemed to get louder every time.

It was a relief when she saw him walk across the office. She feigned nonchalance, pretending to type something as he approached her desk. At first, she feared that he was going to walk straight past her desk and wasn't going to pay any attention to her. But then a bulky shadow moved over her and she looked up, to see him smiling, his blonde hair and his blue eyes, as Viking-like as ever.

"Hello," he said. "I was wondering if I could walk you home again."

She made to talk, coughed, cleared her throat, and then replied: "Okay, yes."

******

They walked the same route they'd walked last night, only this time there

14

was still a hint of sunlight in the sky, and the streetlamps had yet to be turned on. The sun peeked through grey clouds and made the rain-covered streets glisten faintly. They said nothing to each other for a few minutes, and Eliza was worried she was boring him, but then Gregory smiled and said: "I hope you don't think my kissing you was presumptuous… In truth, I just couldn't help myself."

"Not at all."

"I get the sense that you've never taken many risks in your life. I get the sense that you've always been the 'quiet girl'. I get the sense that you've played this role for so long you even see yourself that way. When we get to your apartment, I want you to invite me in. I have a proposition for you. At first it will seem crazy, but I think the more you think about it, the more it will make sense."

"What proposition?" Eliza asked, confused and slightly scared all at once.
"Not here," Gregory said, gesturing at the street in general. "There are too many hum—people around."

Eliza agreed and they carried on towards her apartment. At some point Gregory had taken her hand. Eliza couldn't remember when. It seemed so natural for their hands to be intertwined that she hadn't questioned it. It was only when he gave her hand a squeeze that she realized they were holding hands. His hand was warm and big, and strong. He squeezed her hand and then brought it to his lips and kissed it. He kissed her arm, up and up, and then let it drop. The phantom impression of his kisses lingered on her skin for a long time.

"Tell me about yourself," Eliza said. "I've told you about myself. Tell me about yourself."

"What do you want to know?"
Eliza grinned. "A story from your childhood."
Gregory smiled at her. Eliza felt like she had won something, then; she was sure, by the way he smiled, that he had never had his own question asked back at him before. "Hmm," he said. "I'm not sure."
"What about Ireland? That's where you're from, isn't it?"
"How could you tell?"
"You're joking."
"Perhaps."
"Tell me a story from your childhood," she repeated, more forcefully than was like her.
He nodded, chewed his lip as he thought it over, and then spoke in a wistful voice.
"When I was a boy, we were always poor. My father ran out when my

brothers and I were very young, so it was just us and our mother. Our mother took to drink to make it easier. I used to hate her for that. But now I see why she did it. The world is a cruel place and drink made it easier for her. But some of the boys in the village, and at school, knew that our mother drank, and they loved to torment her.

"They would throw stones at the house and wait for Mother to come out, and then shout things at her. My brothers and I would chase them, but the cowards would always run away. We never knew exactly who did it, because they didn't have the balls to say it to our faces.

"But one day, when my mother went out, one of these boys thought it would be funny to throw a stone at my mother. It hit her in the head and she fell and bled all over the patio—"

"That's awful!" Eliza exclaimed.

"—All over the patio. Usually, we'd stop chasing them after a while, after we'd made our point. But we weren't going to let this one go. We made the youngest brother wait and we chased the bastard until our lungs felt like they were going to explode. When we caught up with him…" He stopped, and rubbed his eyes with his thumbs. "I think I've chosen a bad story."

"No," Eliza said. "I want to know what happens."

"You will think less of me."

"I don't care."

Gregory sighed, and then went on: "When we caught up with him, we stripped him naked and threw him in a nearby pond. It was December, and the water was iced over. We left him there like that, screaming at him that he should never touch our mother again, and if he ever did he'd get worse than cold water.

"We were terrified that we'd killed him when we got home, and wouldn't leave the house for days. But it was okay. He'd walked a mile to his house. He was okay. He survived. But only because he was a mean bastard, and he wanted his revenge. But that day never came. He was a coward, that boy. A mean coward."

Gregory looked into her eyes. "You think less of me."

"He hurt your mother," Eliza said.

"He could've died."

Eliza didn't reply to this. She couldn't think of anything to say.

Once again, they were standing outside her apartment building.

"Invite me in," he said.

"Okay," she said, without thinking. "Please, come in".

Gregory followed close behind her as they ascended the steps. His body was close to hers and he breathed on her neck. This would've been creepy, had anyone else done it, but when Gregory did it Eliza felt excited. He kissed her neck, and then put his arm around her and grabbed her breasts over her shirt when they were at the door.

"Open the door," he said, when she hesitated for a few moments. "Open it, now."

She put the key in the lock and turned it, and it was as though the click marked another epoch in her life. She had just transitioned from the shy, quiet girl to the girl who gets felt up in the hallway by a mysterious Irish man. She walked across the apartment and he followed her, touching her all the way. His hands went down the front of her shirt and touched her breasts underneath. He squeezed the nipple and twisted it. It hurt, but it felt good, too.

He bit her neck and kissed her skin and grabbed her neck with his hand. His breathing got quicker and Eliza felt as though she were in the presence of an animal who would soon lose control. She disentangled herself from him – reluctantly – and sat on the couch. He sat beside her without the least hint of embarrassment.

"You have a proposition for me?" she said.

He nodded, and his eyes – wild with excitement and lust – dimmed a little. He took a deep breath, as though getting himself under control, and then spoke. The more he spoke, the more Eliza felt like she was in a dream, and reality no longer had any meaning.

"Everyone has secrets," he said. "Some people's secrets—Most people's secrets are fairly mundane. The devoted husband and religious man who is addicted to pornography, or the male feminist who secretly masturbates over his feminist friends, or vegetarian who sometimes eats a burger when he's in a different city. My secret, though… It's stranger.

"I'm a werewolf, Eliza."

Eliza laughed. That seemed like the only thing she could do in such a situation. She thought it was a joke. No, she knew it was a joke. That was the only explanation for something so strange. When she laughed, she expected him to laugh with her. They would both have a good laugh about it together, because it was such a strange thing to say. But he wasn't laughing. He was looking at her seriously.

"You're joking," she said. "Obviously, you're joking."

"I'm not," he said. "I'm telling the truth."

"Werewolves aren't real," she said.

"They are."

"They're not."

"They are."

"They are not."

Now it was Gregory's turn to laugh. "You don't have to believe me," he said. "You just have to listen to my request."

Suddenly, Eliza was angry. How dare he come in here and try to make a fool of her! She shot to her feet and pointed at the door. "Get out," she growled. "Get out of here right now."

Gregory got to his feet and stood next to her. "No," he said. "I won't."

"Yes," Eliza said. "You will."

But already some of the fury was seeping from Eliza.

"You want proof," Gregory said. "That's fine. As it gets closer to the full moon, I start to get some wolf-like abilities. My sense of smell, for example, gets much better. But there's an easier way to show you... I get quicker. Watch."

She started to protest, but he held up a hand. "Just humor me."

She sighed and sat back down. He walked across the room, to the far end of the room. "Watch closely," he said. She watched as he crouched, and then—He was at the other end of the room.

Her mouth fell open. "What the..."

And then he was back where he started. She saw something, a flicker, a nebulous haze of movement, but it was too fast for her eyes to comprehend. "How did you do that?" she said.

He walked over to her and sat beside her. "I have shared my secret with you," he said.

"Why?"

"Because I want you to stop playing the shy girl. I've watched you since I worked there, Eliza. That's the truth."

"You stalked me?"

"Watched. I never followed you home, but whenever I came into your department I paid special attention to you. I know there's something underneath that shy exterior. Am I wrong?"

"I don't know," Eliza said. "I have no idea who I am."

That was an odd thing to say, and only after Eliza had said it did she realize how odd it was.

"Most people don't," Gregory said. "But that's fine, because I know who you are."

"And who's that?"

"Someone special," he said, and then kissed her, hard, on the lips.

Their lips mashed together and then they were walking to the bedroom together.

CHAPTER 4

Their sex was greedy and quick. Gregory pushed her onto the bed and ripped her clothes off, and threw them to the ground. Eliza looked up at him as he took off his clothes. His torso was covered in faded pink scars that bulged under his impressive muscles. He leaned over her and kissed her lips, and then he was inside of her.

He thrust deep and hard inside of her, pushing himself deep into her pussy, pounding into her g-spot. She moaned loudly – she had never been fucked like this – and scratched his back. She left deep gouges in his skin as he thrust in and out of her. The heat between her legs was fire-like, and then she felt her pussy go tight around his cock. His rock-hard, huge cock that hurt her but pleasured her at the same time. Her pussy went tight around his cock and she came all over it.

He pushed into her tightened pussy and bit her neck. He whispered in her ear: "You're my dirty fucking slut. You're my dirty little fucking whore. You're my tight little hole."

"Yes, yes," she moaned.

"Tell me what you are," he commanded.

"I'm a fucking whore, I'm a fucking slut, I'll be whatever you want."

She was about to wrap her legs around him. Her fingers were getting deeper and deeper into his strong back. But then he flipped her over so she was on her front. He lifted her and put her knees on the bed, and then pushed her head down so her ass was poking upwards. He pushed his cock inside of her and pounded into her pussy. She moaned and pushed back on his cock, gripping the edge of the bed with her hands, pushing with her arms and moving her hips.

He moaned loudly, and fucked her quicker and harder. "Fuck, fuck, fuck," he breathed, and his hands opened and closed on her ass. "Fuck, yes, fuck. You're a dirty fucking whore, aren't you?"

"Yes," she squealed, as he fucked her harder than she'd even been fucked—harder than she'd ever thought she would get fucked.

He kept grabbing her ass, and then he exploded inside of her. As he came, her pussy got tight again and electric pleasure coursed through her body. She panted as the pleasure moved through her, and his come shot into her, and as his cock wilted her orgasm passed and she fell forward, wondering what the hell just happened. Sex had never taken her with such passion before.

"Oh my god," she sighed, and her eyes were heavy.

Gregory lay beside her. "I know," he said.

She curled up as his come spilled out of her. "What was your request, anyway?"

"I want you to fuck me when I'm in werewolf form," he said. "Tomorrow night, I want you to fuck a werewolf."

"Yes," she mumbled, already half-asleep. "Yes, that sounds good."
******

When she woke, Gregory was dressed and writing in a notepad. "Do you remember what you agreed to?" he said.

She looked at the clock. It was almost midnight. "Yes," she said. "I remember."

She wasn't sure how she had agreed to such a strange request, but she had now... and she had to admit she was curious. Earlier she had had sex she hadn't thought was possible; and now she had the opportunity for the strangest, most alien sex anybody had even had (that she knew of).

"I'm writing the address of the place I change in on this piece of paper," he said. "I'm going to leave a key, too. Tomorrow night – at 11.p.m. – I want you to go there and let yourself in. We've already had sex, so my werewolf-self will know not to hurt you. But he will be very, very horny. He'll smell the sex on you."

"Okay—Wait, is that the only reason you had sex with me?"

He laughed. "Don't be stupid. It was amazing."

"Okay. Good."

He finished scribbling in the pad and then laid a key beside the paper. "I'm going to go now," he said, and looked out the window at the moon. "Tomorrow, I won't be myself. Are you sure you can handle this, Eliza?"

"I don't know," Eliza said, honestly. "It's all happening so fast, but I'm going to be there. I'd regret it forever if I didn't come."

"Good," Gregory said.

And then he left. She got up to see him out, but he was already out of the bedroom, and then the she heard the door close from outside and she was alone again. She picked up the notepad and studied the address. It was the address of a house on the outskirts of the city. Eliza searched it on the internet, so she would recognize it tomorrow.

All the while, a voice was whispering: Are you really going to do this? Seriously? Are you really going to put yourself at risk like this? Anyway, you don't even know that he's what he says he is. It's far more likely that you're going crazy.

This voice was making sense, but she still ignored it. She had ignored sense thus far – she had walked home with a stranger and let a stranger in her home; she had had sex with a stranger – and it had brought her excitement and pleasure. Maybe Gregory was right. Maybe there was more to her.

The house was a mansion in the middle of a country road. "So," she said, into the darkness. "This is where I'll lose my werewolf-virginity."

She laughed, and then turned on all the lights in the apartment.

When her apartment was sufficiently bright, she sat in the living room with a glass of wine and stared into nothing. She was trying to process all that had happened over the past couple of days, but it was hard. Until now her life had been a steady routine.

Now that routine was changing drastically.

The thing that scared her most was she welcomed the change

CHAPTER 5

Eliza was terrified when she drove to the outskirts of the city. Darkness was all around her and she kept thinking that her car would break down and she would be left, stranded, waiting for whatever horrors came along that night to do terrible things to her. She kept thinking of every horror movie she'd ever seen, and imprinting them on her own life. She knew thinking like this wouldn't help her, in any way, but she couldn't help it. She just kept thinking and thinking of all the terrible things that would happen to her. It didn't help that the car was rarely used – her work was close to her apartment – and she kept expecting it to break down with every chug and screech. Finally, she got to the mansion. It sat in the middle of a field, surrounded by acres of unused farmland. She drove into the driveway and turned off the engine. When she got out, she half-expected something to reach out from under the car and grab her.

But there was nothing to stop her from walking towards the mansion. Ivy crept up its old-stone walls and wrapped around the pillars that framed the door. She took out the big, ornate key Gregory had given her and unlocked the door. The door was old and oak, so old she thought it would break when she pushed it open. But it only creaked loudly and then she was in the mansion. It was lit with candles that lined the walls, small, flickering flames that threw up shadows of the furniture and bookcases that filled the big entrance room into which she walked.

Before closing the door behind her, she looked into the sky. The moon was full and gleaming.

She closed the door and walked where the candles led. The candles were not lit everywhere in the place. They formed a lit passageway. She followed down the hallway – lined with old-looking pictures – and came to a big, ornate, wooden door. She put her ear against it. She could hear soft growling from the other side.

She took a deep breath, and then opened the door.
The thing she saw had obviously once been Gregory. It was tall and muscular, like him, but whereas Gregory only had a faint beard, this thing was covered in blonde hair. Muscles bulged from under the blonde hair. Eliza chided herself: Not it… him, he, his.
He sniffed the air, and then looked at her. His teeth, too, were larger – saber-like teeth – and Eliza knew, had he wanted to, he could crush her skull in one bite. Never in her life had she felt so powerless.
She stood, frozen, as the werewolf walked across the room.
Part of her wanted to scream, but she thought that might startle him. So she just stood statue-still as the werewolf sniffed her body.
******

The werewolf sniffed her neck, and then nibbled it. She felt the huge teeth on her neck, and she knew that if he bit down just a bit harder he would pierce her flesh and she would bleed out. But he nibbled her softly and then moved his paw over her breasts. The nails were long, but he only used his hairless palm. He wasn't a wolf; he stood upright and there were hairless patches, on his palms and his feet and around his cock. And his cock was still Gregory's. She recognized it instantly.
The werewolf let out a low growl and rubbed her breasts more. Eliza was still frozen, but as he rubbed her breasts she felt her nipples harden and her pussy getting wet. She let out a moan, and this seemed to spur the werewolf on. With a skillful nail, he cut away her t-shirt. It fell away and landed on the floor. He cut her bra away and her pert breasts spilled free.
Eliza moved a little, the lust overriding her fear, and touched the tip of his cock. He let out a grrrrr and moved his cock closer to her. She grabbed the shaft and moved her hand up and down on it, and he nibbled her neck a bit harder. She winced as he pricked the flesh and a bead of blood slid down her skin. She grabbed his cock harder, and moved her hand up and down faster.

The werewolf put his head back and let out a low howl. Then he kicked Eliza's legs from underneath her. She landed on the ground with a thwack. Her head rocked. As she climbed to her knees, the werewolf pushed his cock in her face, and growled insistently. She put the cock in her mouth.

The werewolf whined at this, in pleasure. He pawed her head and pushed his cock into the back of her throat. She choked and tried to pull away, but he fucked her mouth. She relented and grabbed the fur on his legs, grabbed it hard, and then pulled on it and pushed her head down on his cock. It hit the back of her throat, and she gagged, but she fought the gag and kept on. Everything she was doing now was completely out-of-character. But she wasn't thinking of that. She was thinking of the way his cock filled her mouth, and the whines of the werewolf. She licked around the tip and the shaft as the cock filled her mouth. She massaged his balls with one hand and grabbed his ass with the other. His ass was firm and tensed under her hand.

She kept sucking, and her choking sounds filled the room, and then the werewolf pulled his cock away and nudged her head with his leg. She span around, and the werewolf tugged at her pants. He ripped them away and then tore her underwear away with his teeth.

Eliza moaned as she felt the strength of him press down on her back. Her arms strained and then the werewolf's cock was inside of her. He growled in her ear and fucked her hard. There was so much buildup; here was an animal and he wanted to take her hard and rough straightaway.

Eliza pushed back against his thrusts, and his cock filled her pussy. She felt her lips stretching around his huge cock. He scratched down her back, softly at first, and then so hard than blood dripped down the sides of her. But she didn't care. She was too consumed with the pleasure.

The werewolf howled as he fucked her, and when Eliza turned her head she saw he was in a position that a man would've found impossible. His legs were nearly beside her head, and his body was hunched over her—his hips stretched back, away from his body. It was a position that meant he could put his whole strength and weight into each thrust.

He pounded into her pussy, and then, so quick she barely had time to register it, she came. It was a quick orgasm, and passed quickly. It rushed through her like a wave and then departed. The werewolf carried on, completely oblivious of her pleasure. She knew this beast only saw her as a hole to fuck, and she didn't care. In fact, this was part of the pleasure. Without warning, the werewolf pulled out of her and kicked her in the leg, so she was on her back. She knew, then, that he wasn't just an animal: an animal would never fuck in this position. He lifted her with his paws, his nails scratching her, and she wrapped her legs around him. He stood upright and pushed his cock inside of her.

She wrapped her arms around his shoulders and bounced up and down on his cock. His shoulder muscles shifted beneath her forearms. She was close to his face now, and, despite the darkness, she could see that his irises were the same blue; and she could've sworn there was a hint of Gregory in them. Then she was moving too fast as he lost control and fucked her harder and harder. He growled in her face, through gritted teeth. She came again, this time harder—squirting on his huge cock. He grabbed her ass with his paws, cutting the flesh, and pushed inside of her faster and faster.

Then he fell back, and she fell atop him. She rode him as he pushed upwards, grabbing her neck with his paws. She rode him, and then she felt his cock engorge inside of her, and then the werewolf was howling. She could see the veins on his neck pushing outwards, and his powerful teeth gleaming in the low moonlight that came in through the windows.

Then he was coming; and she came with him. She writhed, and his cock was going soft inside of her. The werewolf pushed her away. She slid from him and sat on the floor, her pussy aching with heat and the force with which he'd fucked her.

After a while, the werewolf crawled over to her and laid his head in her lap, moaning softly. She lay back, and, after stroking the werewolf behind the ears for a few minutes, she slept.

CHAPTER 6

When she woke, it was still dark. She was freezing cold. She found her clothes and wrapped up in them, and brought some of the candles in and placed them around the room. On the floor, where the werewolf had been, Gregory lay, naked, breathing softly. She kissed his brow and, after she was warm, walked around the house looking for a blanket. She found one in a big bedroom – probably the master – and brought it back to the room in which Gregory lay.

She checked her watch and saw that it was five a.m., on Saturday. She walked to the window and saw that the moon was now obstructed by thick black clouds. She returned to Gregory and lay the blanket over him.

As she lay there, beside this man who had been a werewolf only a few hours ago, she thought about the dark. She had always been scared of the dark, terrified of it. But now… As she'd walked through the house, she hadn't been scared, not anymore. Something had changed within her. The shadows no longer held that potent fear they'd held her entire life. Instead, they held a potential.

She thought it was because of the werewolf, and Gregory. She had thought the darkness within people was confusing and impossible to decipher. But she had got underneath Gregory, hadn't she? And she'd discovered something amazing. She'd fucked a werewolf. She almost couldn't believe it.

And once you'd fucked a werewolf – a scary dark-lurker – what else was there to be afraid of?

******

When Eliza woke for the second time, Gregory was standing at the window. She looked at his tight ass for a moment, and then walked over to the window and looked out with him. Together they looked at the rolling hills, and the long, empty fields.

"This was my father's house," he said. "I never knew him, but he left me this house. Does that make up for him not being there? Of course not. But it's a nice place, isn't it? I've held off from moving in because it feels too... fake, somehow. How could the man who made me have owned a place like this, when I grew up in a tiny house in Ireland? It's bizarre."

"Everything's bizarre, lately," Eliza said.

He turned to her, and touched her face. And though she'd liked the touch of the paw, she liked the touch of his hand even more. "You did well last night," he said.

"How do you know?"

"I was there..."

"But it wasn't you."

"No, I know, but I was watching."

Eliza thought on this, and then she fell into Gregory's arms. He kissed the top of her head.

The werewolf and the girl stood like that for a long time, and then lust overcame them—

LETTER FROM THE AUTHOR:

I HOPE YOU ENJOYED THIS STORY AS MUCH I ENJOYED WRITING IT.

LET ME WHAT YOU THINK BY LEAVING REVIEW.

I'LL BE RELEASING NEW BOOK IN BEGINNING OF APRIL SO STAY IN LOOP!

LOVES,

ABBY RAINE

Printed in Dunstable, United Kingdom